The Grumpy Goat

Heather Amery

Illustrated by Stephen Cartwright

Language consultant: Betty Root
Series editor: Jenny Tyler

There is a little yellow duck to find on every page.

This is Apple Tree Farm.

This is Mrs. Boot, the farmer. She has two children, called Poppy and Sam, and a dog called Rusty.

Ted works on the farm.

He tells Poppy and Sam to clean the goat's shed.
"Will she let us?" asks Sam. "She's so grumpy now."

Gertie the goat chases Sam.

She butts him with her head. He nearly falls over.
Sam, Poppy and Rusty run out through the gate.

Poppy shuts the gate.

They must get Gertie out of her pen so they can get to her shed. "I have an idea," says Sam.

Sam gets a bag of bread.

"Come on, Gertie," says Sam. "Nice bread."
Gertie eats it and the bag, but stays in her pen.

"Let's try some fresh grass," says Poppy.

Poppy pulls up some grass and drops it by the gate. Gertie eats it but trots back into her pen.

"I have another idea," says Sam.

"Gertie doesn't butt Ted. She wouldn't butt me if
I looked like Ted," says Sam. He runs off again.

Sam comes back wearing Ted's clothes.

He has found Ted's old coat and hat. Sam goes
into the pen but Gertie still butts him.

"I'll get a rope," says Poppy.

They go into the pen. Poppy tries to throw the rope over Gertie's head. She misses.

Gertie chases them all.

Rusty runs out of the pen and Gertie follows him.
"She's out!" shouts Sam. "Quick, shut the gate."

Sam and Poppy clean out Gertie's shed.

They sweep up the old straw and put it in the
wheelbarrow. They spread out fresh straw.

Poppy opens the gate.

"Come on, Gertie. You can go back now," says Sam.
Gertie trots back into her pen.

"You are a grumpy old goat," says Poppy.

"We've cleaned out your shed and you're still grumpy," says Sam. "Grumpy Gertie."

Next morning, they meet Ted.

"Come and look at Gertie now," says Ted. They all
go to the goat pen.

Gertie has a little kid.

"Oh, isn't it sweet," says Poppy. Gertie doesn't look grumpy now," says Sam.

Cover design by Hannah Ahmed   Digital manipulation by Natacha Goransky
This edition first published in 2004 by Usborne Publishing Ltd, 83-85 Saffron Hill, London EC1N 8RT, England. www.usborne.com